The Great Money Tree
An Adventure Begins

Written by Gina Stern
Illustrated by C. Johnson

Dedicated to Judith Hayes

I see Judith Hayes as a bridge and a champion of creativity who helped to move my book forward. Judith is a woman of vision who could see the connection between myself and Cheryl Johnson the illustrator of this book. Judith recognized the connection between two strangers and believed enough in her vision to carry my book to Cheryl and Cheryl's drawings to me. Judith is so lovely and I believe that she was in the right place at the right time. It was an absolute stroke of fortune that brought me to you Cheryl Johnson. In this case fortune's name is Judith Hayes- Gina Stern

Word from the Illustrator
Friendship is a lot of things to different people. Sometimes life events fall like dominoes in a cosmic calculation that supports what was simply meant to be. I've been lucky to call Judith Hayes my friend for some time, and through her loving support and nurturing spirit I was introduced to Gina. Friends are gifts we give ourselves. It's a rare privilege to be associated with such a wonderful project, thanks to Judith, who saw the opportunity to make connections for two people would have otherwise never met. Thank you. Cheryl Johnson

Acknowledgements

I would like to thank my sons Maddox and Beckham for their countless challenges that inspire me to find creative solutions as a parent. Maddox and Beckham, you are my constants. I am blessed to have you in my life and value your insight, collaboration, creativity and zest for life. You keep me current and remind me continually of how amazing life is.

A special thanks to the children of 2G class of 2011, Isaiah, MJ, Caroline, Jason, Ahren, Bridget, Danny, Erin, Jack, Kimberly, Alexis, Julia, Bryant, Kate "The Great", Cole, Joseph, Matthew, Brenna, Ivan and Maddox, for their inspiration and creative energy, you are the original True North Guardians. To Mrs. Iskenderian for your support and trust in my vision. To Mrs. Gallione for sharing your classroom and support. To Marilyn and Karl Tomaso for your constant support and encouragement. A very special appreciation to Cheryl Johnson for your amazing illustrations. To Phyllis for being "half mom, half amazing." Mom, you took the time to teach me how to dream.

Editor - Judith Hayes

There are many characters in this book:

Maddox
Begins the story with one wish

Beckham
Maddox's younger brother and collaborator

Mom
Half mom Half magic

The Great Money Tree

Simon
The leader of the Money Blossom Guardians

Quetzales
Money Blossom Guardian from another land

The children of 2G
The True North Guardians

Table of Contents

The True North Guardians

Part 1

On an ordinary day in an ordinary home, a boy possessed a vision. In his mind's eye, he saw a bright red hoverboard and so the adventure of The Great Money Tree began.

Chapter 1

"Please" and "Can I Have?"

Maddox was convinced that this new red hoverboard would change his life. He decided to ask his mom to buy it for him. "Mom! Mom! Can I have a new hoverboard?" he shouted. Maddox's mother was used to these request, and she sighed heavily, for she knew what was about to begin.

"Maddox!" she said. "You don't eat your vegetables, you hit your brother, and you don't go to bed on time. Why should I buy you a new hoverboard?" Maddox's mom paused to wait for his brilliant explanation of why he deserved this great gift.

Maddox fired back in rapid succession. "Mom, I'll stop hitting my brother, I'll eat all my veggies, and I'll go to bed on time." Smiling, as though she was convinced, Maddox waited for his mother's "Yes." Instead of hearing what he expected, he found himself on the receiving end of a "We'll see." Impatient, bored, and tortured by his visions of red hoverboards dancing in his head, Maddox enlisted the help of his younger brother Beckham.

The boys plotted countless ways to convince their mom to buy them the new hoverboard. They waited until the next day. Like two well-trained army men, they executed their strategy. They descended on their mother for the next round of "Please" and "Can I have?" Clever Maddox went directly for the win. "OK, Mom, I ate my broccoli, I went to bed on time, and I LOVE my brother!" he said. He threw his arms around Beckham for special effect. "Can I have the hoverboard now?" Maddox said with a big smile.

Mom, an all-time veteran of the skirmishes of "Please" and "Can I have?" fired back with a firm "Mommy has to work hard for the money we need. Maybe you can have your new red hoverboard for Christmas."

Deterred, but not daunted, the boys retreated to their room to hatch the next plot in their round of "Please "and "Can I have?" Back in their room, the boys stared impatiently at all the toys on the shelf, but they could only think of one thing; the red hoverboard. In the next round, the boys thought that a tag team aproach would work best on their mom. Maddox was up first. He waited until his mom was nice and distracted, thinking he would get a YES! "Mom, can I have that new hoverboard? I'm so bored with my old toys," Maddox said. Next it was Beckham's turn. "Yeah, Mom. We really need the hoverboard. It will help us ride fast and learn new tricks. We could get everywhere really quickly. It'll help us share, and it will even teach us to have good balance," explained Beckham. Realizing that there was no way out of this reasoning, their mom decided to try a different strategy.

"Boys, if you truly want your new hoverboard, you're going to have to plant a money tree," said their mom. "What's a money tree?" the boys asked. This could be the answer they were waiting for! "Well," Mom said," first you have to get coins which will be the seeds for the money tree. Then you plant the coins. Your tree will grow all the money you need for your new hoverboard."

Excited, the boys jumped at the opportunity to plant seeds for their new money tree. They gathered up their coins, dusted off the shovels and ran to the base of the tree in the backyard. They quickly started planting the money seeds. Once the seeds were planted, the boys went to bed early so they could wake up to a blooming money tree.

Morning came and the boys rushed down the stairs at breakneck speed. They flung the door open, expecting to find all the money they needed for their hoverboard. But there was no money, it was the same old tree where they had buried their coins.

Chapter 2

The Things We Do For Trees

Disappointed, the boys went back to their room to watch the tree from their window. Just then they noticed the landscaper mowing the lawn around their tree. They were sure he had done something sinister to their money tree. In reality, his only crime was caring for the lawn and removing the leaves. But that's not the way the boys saw it.

The boys went to mom for some answers. Their vision of a tree full of money was fading in their minds. "Mom, is there really such a thing as a money tree?" they both asked in harmony. "We waited all night! We woke up this morning to see our money tree but nothing happened. It's exactly the same way we left it," said Maddox. "Boys," Mom smiled, "you have to sing for the tree, and water the tree and, you have to dance for the tree. Only then will your money tree grow."

Maddox and Beckham, with a renewed belief in their dream, tore out of the door and ran up to the tree. Maddox began dancing for it while Beckham watered it and sang his version of "Happy."

Night turned into day, day turned in to night, and the days turn into weeks. Weeks soon became months, months became seasons, and the seasons continued to change. All the while the boys cared for the tree and crafted daily variety shows to convince the tree to grow.

Chapter 3

The Great Money Tree

One spring day, as the boys returned home from school, they were struck by an awesome sight. The tree had transformed. There was a glow that fell from the sky and washed over the tree. It radiated sunbeams, and the roots appeared to have gained muscles that ripped from the ground!

Flower blossoms covered the entire tree. Full of excitement, the boys stared at the tree, just knowing that all of their love, patience and nurturing had finally worked. There was money everywhere!

The boys plucked the money from the tree in a frenzy. They filled their book bags and pockets until every bill they could reach was in hand. "Mom! Mom!" the boys yelled as they burst into the house, "The money tree! It grew!" they exclaimed.

"Wow boys!" said Mom with a smile, "you have all the money you need for your new hoverboard! Do you want to go buy it now?" "No way, Mom!" shouted the boys in unison. "Do you know how long it took us to grow this money? We are going to save it!" The boys spent the rest of the day sorting and separating the money, piling it into high stacks, and then knocking them over. Beckham even made a nest out of his money pile and took a short nap.

Chapter 4

Mom! Mom! Where's My Money Tree?

The next day at school, Maddox and Beckham told all of their friends about the existence of the great Money Tree. They shared the details of how they planted the coin seeds at the base of the tree. They explained how they sang, danced, and watered the tree. They told their classmates how in time the tree blossomed with all of the money they needed for their hoverboard. The boys explained how the tree continued to blossom.

That day the school was all a buzz with stories of The Great Money Tree. Children whispered in every corridor and classroom. When the other schoolchildren returned to their homes after school, they checked their own backyards to see if they had their own money tree growing. When none of the children could find one, they began to ask their parents why they couldn't have a money tree.

That evening, before bedtime, the boy's classmates asked their parents to drive them to Maddox and Beckham's house so they could see the tree for themselves. After a few days, passing by the house to see the tree became a regular ritual for all of the neighborhood children. Word spread so quickly that even the local news came out to cover the story of The Great Money Tree.

Chapter 5

Crowd Control

Soon, word of the tree spread far and wide. Now, instead of planting their own trees or taking tours of The Great Money Tree, people started to imagine ways to take the money from the tree itself. One day, a huge crowd descended on the tree in what can only be described as a mob scene. People began pushing and shoving. Others were arguing, and the crowd began ripping and tearing at the tree until all of the money was gone.

A dark cloud descended over the town and overwhelming sadness filled the children's hearts. The children were sad when they realized that spreading the word about the tree brought out the crowd's greed and caused them to take the money from the tree. The sad children went to bed early that night.

Chapter 6

True North Guardians

Weeks passed, and the Tree showed little signs of life. Maddox and Beckham's mom was asked to come into the school to talk to the children about the Tree. The children still had many questions. One child wanted to know why the Tree grew in the first place and why the trees they planted didn't grow money. Was the Tree really dead? Could the Tree be brought back to life? Ms. Stern, as she was known to most of the children, began her talk by asking the children an important question.

"If you could plant a money tree, and the tree could grow enough money for anything you wanted, what would you ask for?" The children began to call out. "I would build the world's largest roller coaster!" Another boy said "I would buy Jetpacks and fly all around the world!" And then a voice from the back called out "I would buy an airplane and put a bunch of houses on it. I would fly that plane to Haiti and drop all of the houses, because they need houses since the earthquake came. "

Ms. Stern said, "Now that we know what you would do with the money from the Tree. I can tell you that the Tree is not dead, but the Tree will grow only for those who are pure of heart."

Free Puppies
MUST GO TODAY!
Animal Shelter
Tomorrow

"With its special magic, the Tree can detect a person's TRUE NORTH," Ms. Stern said. A voice called out from the back. "What IS our TRUE NORTH?" Ms. Stern explained. "Your TRUE NORTH is a place deep inside of you. TRUE NORTH knows good from bad and right from wrong. Your TRUE NORTH was placed in you before you were born. It's the purest piece of your heart that helps you to understand your fellow man. It's a place inside of you that starts to tear when a tragedy occurs, and it triggers a smile at the sight of a butterfly. TRUE NORTH is present in every child on earth." She continued to explain, "The Tree can only be planted and nurtured by children, because they have the purest hearts." The children hung on her every word. "Over time" she went on, "and as we get older, we slowly begin to lose our TRUE NORTH." Ms. Stern looked intently at the children as she explained, "There are very few adult guardians of The Great Money Tree left on earth." Looking into the crowd of children's faces, she pronounced, "Now that the Tree is facing such danger, it is necessary to appoint a new generation of TRUE NORTH GUARDIANS. "

One by one, the children began to stand up. They all wanted to defend the Tree. Together they proclaimed, "I am a TRUE NORTH GUARDIAN!" The children began to transform for their new roles as TRUE NORTH GUARDIANS. Those children who were fast were made faster with sonic speed. They became the Sonics. Those who were strong were made even stronger. They became the Lifters. Those who could jump, could now jump higher. They became the Springers. Soon there were children with laser beams that could shoot from their eyes, and they became the Beamers. Those who could do back flips and somersaults became known as the Aerials. The new generation of the True North Guardians was complete. The Sonics, the Lifters, the Springers, the Beamers, and the Aerials came together with hands united in the air and proclaimed, "We are the True North Guardians!"

Chapter 7

A New Home For The Great Money Tree

The children quickly gathered to discuss their plan for the Tree. Soon it was decided that they would move The Great Money Tree deep into the forest, where only the children with their newfound abilities could find it. The location was kept secret. After the move, daily activities in the forest, with the Tree, were now beginning to follow a regular routine.

Each day the children visited the Tree and sang beautiful songs to it, danced wonderful dances for it, and gave it water to drink. They patiently waited for the day the Money Tree would blossom once again.

Things were happening the same way they did in the beginning. The seasons passed until finally the Money Tree bloomed, only this time it was different!

These new money blossoms had eyes. Upon closer inspection, and with a quick poking, the blossoms began to fly. Soon all of the money blossoms sprang to life. They put on an aerial show of epic proportions. They swirled in the air with precision. They flew in formation and began gliding towards the ground. As the children watched, they couldn't help but notice that as these money blossoms glided they looked like floating dollar bills. Once the money blossoms landed, their leader stepped forward to introduce himself to the children.

He said, "I am Simon. We are the guardians of the Tree. We are here to help you protect The Great Money Tree. We live on the Tree and our coats act as camouflage to help us blend in with the real money blossoms. We scout the skies for danger and will alert you of any intruders."

Chapter 8

Joining Forces

The children spend their days getting acquainted with the Tree's many guardians. Each money blossom was assigned to a team leader. Sonics, known for their speed, paired with the Aerial leaders and took the point position. The acrobats of the True North paired with the jumpers of the money blossoms. Once the guardians were matched with their money blossom counterparts, they began their drills. Life in the forest was filled with song and dance as the guardians waited for the real money blossoms to bloom. Finally, there was new growth on the Tree's branches. The Great Money Tree had come back to life. It was illuminated, and it filled the sky with an enchanting bright glow. Everyone that gazed at the Tree was mesmerized. The guardians approached the tree slowly to inspect the new money blossoms. There were fifty and one hundred dollar bills everywhere. The blossoms completely covered the base of the Tree and grew up the trunk and the branches like ivy. The money blossom guardians began to fly in formation. One by one they took their places among the tree branches. The children were in awe of the spectacle. They could barely tell the money blossom guardians apart from the actual money blossoms. The children knew that all of their efforts had been rewarded. The Tree was now fully alive and well protected.

Chapter 9

A Visitor in the Forest

Suddenly, the money blossom guardians began to swirl. They departed from the Tree and glided into formation. Simon notified the TRUE NORTH GUARDIANS of an intruder. Everyone was on high alert. Off in the distance, barely visible to the naked eye were bright flashes of color. The TRUE NORTH GUARDIANS began to take their positions. Simon and the Sonics took the point as the swirling flashes of color drew nearer. The sky filled with vibrant orange, pink and green. As the flashes got closer, shapes began to appear. It was the recognizable formation and glide of the money blossoms. But, these money blossoms were brilliantly colored in a foreign money pattern. The formation broke and one intruder money blossom took the lead in an aerial spectacle that looked like a dance. The leader glided to a landing and introduced himself.

"My name is Quetzales Gonzalez, and we are the money blossom guardians from Guatemala." Quetzales had reached the Guardian camp with some terrible news. Simon stepped forward and welcomed Quetzales with open arms. The two had met many years ago on a super-secret mission to Brazil. Simon suggested Quetzales rest from his long journey before he told them the news. While Quetzales rested, Simon gathered all the guardians and money blossom protectors so that they could all hear the news together. When Quetzales woke, he told Simon and the children why he had flown over 2000 miles for their help. Quetzales explained," Guatemala is being flooded by heavy rains due to La Niña, and those rains are ruining all of the corn and bean crops. The people grow these crops for food and money, but before the rains came there were serious droughts! The weather extremes are causing many people to go hungry! Things are desperate.

"Quetzales continued," and if that isn't enough, tropical storms are destroying the land. Volcanic eruptions are also forcing people to flee from their homes." Quetzales pleaded with the TRUE NORTH GUARDIANS, "The children of Guatemala need your help and they need it fast!"

The guardians were united in their decision to help the children of Guatemala. They began by collecting money blossoms from their Tree. They packed up all the supplies that were needed and divided themselves into teams to begin their mission. The Springers and the Beamers paired with their money blossom counterparts to guard The Great Money Tree. The Sonics, along with the Lifters and the Aerials, strapped on their jet packs for their long journey to Guatemala. They were ready to help. With Quetzales leading the way, the TRUE NORTH GUARDIANS and the money blossom guardians of Guatemala took flight to bring the magic of the Great Money Tree to all of the Guatemalan children in need.

In time, the TRUE NORTH GUARDIANS along with the money blossom guardians arrived at their destination in Guatemala. Just as they had in the past, when they moved the tree into a secret forest, The TRUE NORTH GUARDIANS began their work to inspire another GREAT MONEY TREE to grow in Guatemala. They were able to bring happiness to many, many children.

About The Great Money Tree

With a strong belief that everyone is entitled to the experiences they want, not just the ones they are dealt, Gina Stern's original intention was to change her own experience around the game of "Please" and "Can I have?" that she found herself presented with daily by her two sons Maddox and Beckham. The Great Money Tree is based on a lesson that she was trying to share with her boys about instant gratification and the pursuit of "stuff." Overtime the story of The Great Money Tree took on a global conversation, when one very important question was asked. If you could plant a Money Tree to grow money for anything you wanted, what would you ask for?

www.thegreatmoneytree.com

Twitter- @greatmoneytree

Now it's *YOUR* turn!

If you could plant a Money Tree, and it could grow money for anything you wanted, what would you ask for?

Who are your TRUE NORTH GUARDIANS?

What special powers would the
     TRUE NORTH GUARDIANS have?

What do the TRUE NORTH GUARDIAN
    uniforms look like?

What is your animal protector?

Where would you bring the power of The Great Money Tree and why?

About the Author

Gina Stern is Puerto Rican and Dominican. She was born and raised in the Bronx, NY. She is the proud mother of two beautiful sons and currently resides in New Jersey.

Gina is widely recognized in the airport industry and press as the pioneer of the airport spa concept. Gina has been featured on Montel Williams, "Rags to Riches" discussing her journey to success from an inner-city youth and high school dropout to college graduate and CEO of a million Dollar enterprise. Gina later went on to receive her BA from Marist College. She also attended the TUCK school of business at Dartmouth and received certification through the MBE program.

Made in the USA
San Bernardino, CA
16 May 2016